One Boy's War

Lynn Huggins-Cooper

Illustrated by Ian Benfold Haywood

F

FRANCES LINCOLN
CHILDREN'S BOOKS

WAR HAS BEEN DECLARED!

The papers are full of the news that the Germans have attacked France.

Pa is restless. His pals are rushing off in droves to join up. He says, "It's every man's duty to fight for King and Country." Ma scowls and clashes the pots together in the kitchen whenever he says that.

I wish I was older. I'll be sixteen just before Christmas. But Pa says the war will be over by then — hope not, not before I get a crack at the Kaiser!

PA'S GONE.
Last night, he crept into my room and told me he was going. He smelt faintly of tobacco and beer as he bent over me. His eyes were shining with excitement.

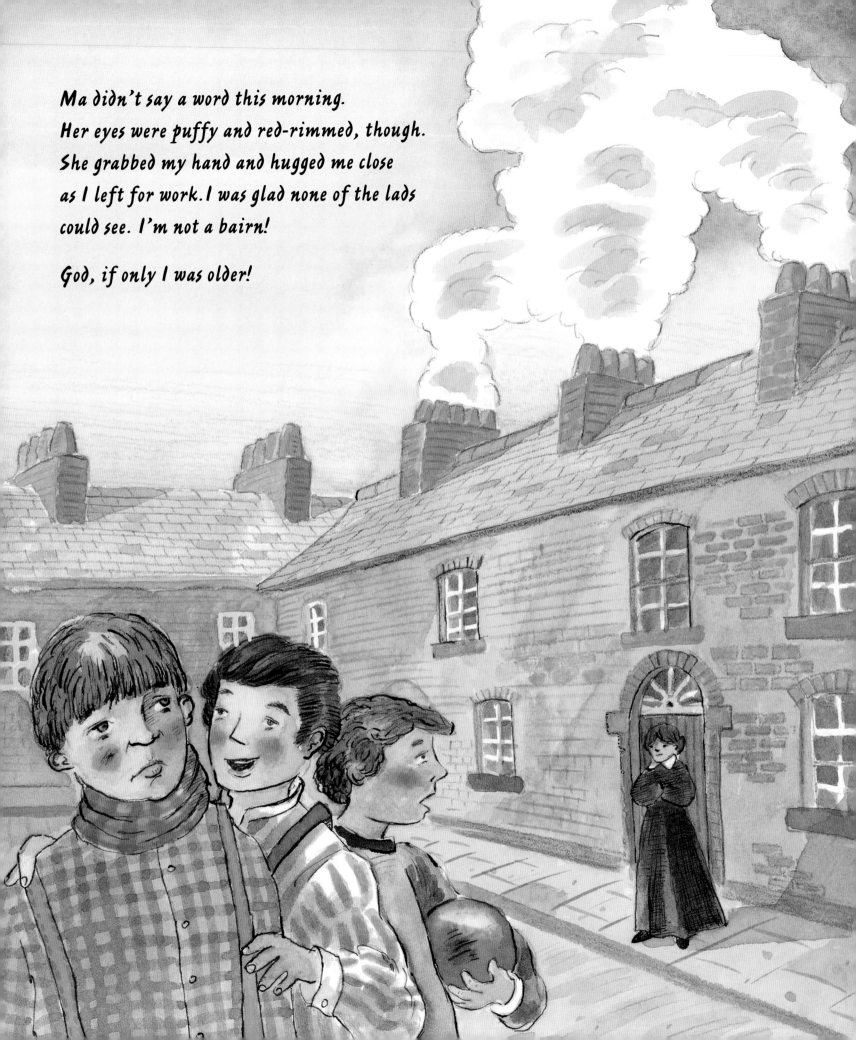

Ma didn't say a word this morning.
Her eyes were puffy and red-rimmed, though.
She grabbed my hand and hugged me close
as I left for work. I was glad none of the lads
could see. I'm not a bairn!

God, if only I was older!

I've made up my mind. I'm joining up.
Ma's smothering me.
From the moment I get in, her eyes are on me.

Everywhere I go I see flags and recruiting stations.
It's like they're calling to me. Pa always said
we should stand up against bullies – and what else
    is the Kaiser, marching into France like that?

    I'll lie about my age.
        I'm tall, so there shouldn't be a problem.

I wonder where Pa is now?
I bet he'll be proud of me.

WELL, I MADE IT!

Bit sticky there for a moment. The recruiting sergeant
eyed me up and down, and smirked when I said I was nineteen.
But he took me anyway.

The training's been hard. I've put on lots of muscles, though!
Don't dare write to Ma yet.

One lad told me he was sixteen. One of the other lads must have said something, because the next thing we knew, his mother turned up at the camp, full of hell!

Poor old Jim was 'claimed out', and the last we saw of him was his mother marching him down the road, boxing his ears as she went. I think Jim's ma could be a one-woman battalion – the Kaiser wouldn't stand a chance!

After that I kept quiet.

Poor Ma.

Hope she found the note I left.

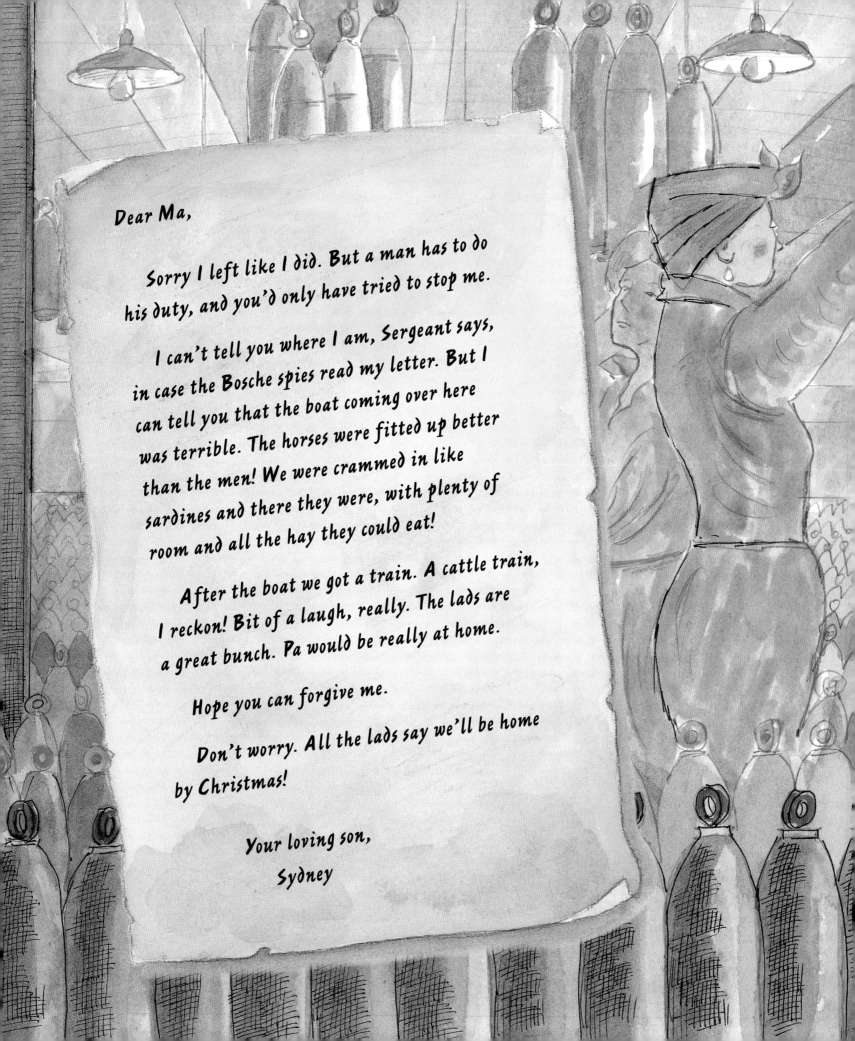

Dear Ma,

Sorry I left like I did. But a man has to do his duty, and you'd only have tried to stop me.

I can't tell you where I am, Sergeant says, in case the Bosche spies read my letter. But I can tell you that the boat coming over here was terrible. The horses were fitted up better than the men! We were crammed in like sardines and there they were, with plenty of room and all the hay they could eat!

After the boat we got a train. A cattle train, I reckon! Bit of a laugh, really. The lads are a great bunch. Pa would be really at home.

Hope you can forgive me.

Don't worry. All the lads say we'll be home by Christmas!

Your loving son,
Sydney

I never thought it would be like this.
When we started to dig the trenches, it still
seemed like a bit of a lark. Good hard work, a smoke, a laugh. Men's work.

But then the rain started. Torrents of it. The trenches are more like
muddy ponds. Yellow, soupy water soaks us as we trudge through
the muddy channels. I bet 'Wipers' was lovely once – green fields
and bird-filled hedges, just like Durham. Not now.

Then the fighting started.

One of the lads took a 'Blighty' today – off home with one leg gone below the knee, poor sod. Blown off by a shell. He's only nineteen. He'll never work again.

Beginning to wish it had been me.

It's the noise that gets to you. The pounding.
Like a thunderstorm that never ends. Then there's the weird
buzzing just over your head. Like angry bees, but with a far
deadlier sting. Bosche bullets, that's what they are.

Jonesy bought it today. One minute he was moaning about
the chloride of lime in the tea — said he wanted to drink it,
not bleach the latrines! Next minute, he was hunched over, coughing.
A horrible bubbling noise was choking up out of his chest.
All I could do was stare. He looked so scared. Then he went quiet.

I'd give anything to be back at home.

God help us if he's listening, which I doubt. I don't know what's worse – the lice or the rats. My clothes are crawling and my skin is red-raw. The itching's terrible. My mate Billy runs a match up the seams of his khaki and you can hear the beggars pop – but there are always more to take their place.

And the rats are so bold. They steal your food in broad daylight! Last night Billy shot one – as big as a cat, I swear it was. Wish I had Toff, my Pa's terrier. He'd show them a thing or two!

Hope Pa's better off than me.
Wonder where he is tonight.

I'm so sick of the wet. No matter how much
we bale the foul water out, it oozes straight back into
the trenches. We're soaked through all the time.
My feet are sore. "Trench Foot", the medic called it.
My feet stink. But all the lads are the same.

A shell hit nearby today. It was the strangest thing I've ever seen.
A wall of mud rose up where the shell hit, and surged towards us.
It broke over our heads like a wave, covering us in mud and stones.

I was talking to Billy when it hit. Our mouths filled with mud.
As I scrubbed my eyes, I caught sight of Billy's wide eyes staring
out of a face as black as the roads. I started laughing, but Billy
just carried on staring.

Poor old Billy. Such a comic. But he'll not be laughing again in this life.

Wish I was back home.

Well, we're waiting for "zero". At 08.45 hours
we'll be going over the top. The guns started pounding hours ago.
Pretty soon, we'll be up the ladders and over.

Please God, make me go. I don't want to let the lads down.
But I'm so scared. You feel so naked, running towards
those guns. Suppose the Bosche feel the same.

I hope there's not a bullet out there
with my name on it.

One of the lads has gone doolally —
crying, rocking, and calling for his ma
like a bairn. Can't blame him.

Every time I shut my eyes, I see myself doing that funny twirling dance you see when a lad goes down under fire.

Wish I was at home with my ma.

Soon, soon.
Won't be long, Ma.

My darling,

I'll be home soon. Injured at Ypres – but don't worry your head, it's just enough to send me home. It's been bad. Really bad.
But it's over now – for me, anyway!

Tell Sydney I'll be home soon. I've missed you both so much. But knowing you both are safe has kept me going.

Your Ever-loving Husband,

Peter

Sydney was a real young man. He was born in County Durham, but died in a muddy field in Belgium. His story is tragic. For millions of young men like Sydney there was no happy ending. Almost every family in Britain, Germany, France and Russia lost someone in the First World War.

At the beginning of the war, 'Pals' Battalions' went to fight together. These groups were made up of all the young men from a particular village or estate. Whole battalions were wiped out, leaving a village desolate, with no young men to return.

Many young boys lied about their age in order to join up. The youngest soldier to die was Private John Condon, who was only fourteen years old. But some soldiers were even younger. James Bartaby was only thirteen when he joined up, as was Myer Rosenblum from London.

Look around your town and see if you can find a war memorial. Read the names, and think about the poor young boys and men who died. Think of all the grieving families who lost them. Your old family photos may show men who fought – and even died – in World War I. Women died too. Many volunteered as nurses and ambulance drivers, living and dying in terrible conditions.